Gift Horse

A Lakota Story

Written and illustrated by S. D. Nelson

Harry N. Abrams, Inc., Publishers

The thing I remember most from my early days is a horse . . . a Gift Horse. My father had been away visiting and trading with our friends, the Cheyenne. When he came home, he rode into camp with some new horses trailing behind him, and our whole village turned out to welcome him. Singling out a pony, he called to me.

"This, my son, is the horse for a boy who is becoming a man . . . and a Lakota Warrior," he said. As the young horse came forward, she nickered and stamped her hooves. She tossed back her head and perked up her ears. She was the blue-gray color of a thunderstorm, and her back was a blur of white spots, like hailstones raining down.

I named my horse Storm. Wakan-Tanka, the Great Spirit who is in all things, had already painted her like a summer hailstorm. With mixed paints I added yellow thunderbolts and placed a red handprint on her hip. I circled her eye with a red band so she would see straight and true.
Finally, I tied eagle feathers in her flowing mane.

We spent all of our days together. I was already a good rider, but on Storm I became like the wind. Across the wide-open prairie we rode, beneath an endless sky of blue. People said the dust we stirred up looked like a flying cloud on the Earth, and so they began to call me Flying Cloud.

There were many games we boys played on horseback. We practiced with our bows and arrows. We wrestled. Sometimes we played rough and were knocked from our horses. I always climbed right back on Storm. This was good training for us because when we became Lakota Warriors, we would need to defend our people from our enemies. Also, we needed to become successful buffalo hunters. If we failed at hunting the buffalo, our people might starve to death during the bitter cold of winter.

Early one morning, I sneaked out of my family's tipi and rode far away from
camp. I knew I was not supposed to go, but I wanted to prove that I could
hunt as well as any man. At first, the snow-covered ground made the fresh deer
tracks easy to follow. But then, North Wind began to blow. I dismounted for a
closer look. Suddenly, three deer appeared. I shot one of my arrows, but my
fingers were cold and I missed. Soon the gusting wind turned into a raging
prairie blizzard. Storm whinnied and nudged me from behind. Her eyes held
a look I had never seen before . . . fear.

My fingers were numb from cold, but somehow I managed to mount Storm.
The snow was blowing so hard that I could not see my hand in front of my
face. "We are lost!" I shouted. I wrapped my arms around my horse's neck.
She was warm, just like my parents' tipi. "Storm, take us home!" I cried.
Together we trudged into the darkness of the blizzard. We wandered
for a long, long time. I was freezing and ready to give up when I
noticed that Storm had stopped. There before us was my family's
tipi. Storm had brought us home. She had saved my life!

That blizzard taught me to think before acting. My mother saw that I had learned an important lesson. She told me that I was becoming a man and that I would soon be ready to wear the shirt of a Warrior. She promised to make one decorated with beadwork and porcupine quills. But I would have to collect the quills! After many days of hunting, I finally found a porcupine. He was bristling with sharp spines. I could have killed him with one of my stone-tipped arrows, but I only needed *some* of his quills. I threw a small blanket across his back. When I pulled it away, the cloth was filled with a forest of quills.

Before my mother could use the quills, she first had to make the shirt. The women and girls of our tribe tanned the animal hides that the hunters brought back to camp. They stitched them together to make many things, including all of our clothing and the lodgeskins for our tipis. That spring, when the little green growing things began to show themselves, my mother and sister began sewing a Warrior's shirt for me. They used a fine antelope hide and decorated it with beads and the porcupine quills.

Also, that spring, to prepare me for becoming a Warrior,
my father took me into the sweat lodge with him. I sat in
a circle with the men of my tribe. Several large stones,
which had been heated in a fire, were brought in
and placed in a pit in the center of the lodge. The
buffalo-skin door flap was closed, and darkness
surrounded us. Old Yellow Bear, the medicine man
of our tribe, used a turtle shell to pour water over
the glowing stones. They hissed and spat. Steam
filled the lodge. In the darkness, the men began
to sing ancient songs that I had never heard
before. It was so hot that sweat flowed down
over my whole body. I felt wonderfully clean.
Yellow Bear told me that I was now ready to
go on a journey of the spirit—a Vision Quest.

I spent four days alone, praying on a distant hillside, without food and water. Sleeping under the stars, I felt the pain of hunger and was very thirsty. I missed Storm. Each day I prayed to Father Sun and Sister Moon, and to the Star People. I asked Wakan-Tanka to teach me the lessons that would make me a strong and good person. On the third night a vision came to me: all of the four-legged creatures like Deer, Coyote, and Buffalo are my brothers. I saw that all of the winged creatures like Hawk and Hummingbird are my sisters. Even the creepy-crawlies like Lizard and Spider are my relatives. I dreamed that, along with all of these creatures, we two-legged beings dance together in the circle of life.

It was time to return to my village. My Vision Quest was over, and I had taken another step toward becoming a man. But I still had not earned the right to wear the shirt of a Lakota Warrior.

On the prairie there were as many buffalo as there are leaves on a tree. My father told me there was no greater honor than providing meat and buffalo robes for our people. The time had come for me to join the men of my tribe in the hunt. I remember how the earth shook under the stampeding hooves. My stomach was upside down with fear and excitement. Then Storm drew up alongside a large bull, and for a moment we were galloping together. I shot my arrows, and they flew straight and true.

Suddenly, before me, a huge buffalo lifted a horse and rider into the air. The bull turned them over onto the earth. The terrified horse bolted away, and I knew the angry buffalo would attack the helpless man. Turning Storm, I galloped to the rescue. We rode up just as the bull charged. With one hand I grasped Storm's neck, and with the other I reached out. Using all of my strength, I swung the man up behind me, and we rode to safety.

Later, as I stood over my first buffalo, I was so proud I howled like a wolf. I knelt down by my Buffalo Brother and thanked him for giving up his life so that my people could eat. I thanked him for his hide and told him it would make a fine robe to keep us warm in the cold of winter.

Many tribes lived on the Great Plains. Some of them, like the Cheyenne, were our friends, but others, like the Crow, were our enemies. Early one morning, while we still slept, Crow horse thieves attacked. I woke up to shouting and the pounding of hooves. Most of our horses were stolen. That morning, as the sun rose in the east, angry tears filled my eyes. How could those thieves dare to steal my precious Storm?

We cut up the meat and wrapped it in the buffalo hides. Everyone helped . . .
men, women, and children. We loaded the bundles onto pony drags and hauled
them all back to our village. As we traveled, my people made up a song. They
sang about how a horse named Storm and a boy called Flying Cloud had rescued
a fallen Warrior from a charging buffalo. My father told me I had a courageous
heart. He said that I was no longer a boy, but that I was not yet a man either.
There was one more thing I needed to do: I had to face the enemy with the heart
of a Warrior. That night we celebrated with a great feast and a Buffalo Dance.

We put together our own raiding party. Our
men planned to get back all our horses and to punish
the thieves by stealing as many Crow ponies as possible.
We traveled on foot, following the trail left by our stolen horses.
I prayed to Wakan-Tanka to return Storm safely to me.

Days later we reached the Crow village. The sky was growing dark,
and a fierce thunderstorm was coming up. At first I was afraid that the storm
would ruin our rescue effort, but then I thought of *my* Storm and knew that
Wakan–Tanka was answering my prayer. The Thunderbeings beat their thun-
der-drums overhead and threw spears of lightning to the earth. Rain poured
down, soaking us to the bone but allowing us to sneak up on our enemies.

West Wind roared in the treetops as we drew near our beloved horses. The men from my tribe dashed to the rescue. Hail pelted my face and shoulders. Lightning flashed as bright as day. In the glare, I saw my Storm and the Crow Warrior who stood guarding her! Thunder pounded overhead. I prayed for courage and raced to my horse. Lightning flashed again as I knocked over the Crow guard and jumped up on Storm. With my fingers clutching her mane, we disappeared into the wild night. I felt a Crow arrow whiz past my ear, but I never looked back. Yelping like a coyote, I helped chase the entire horse herd back home. The night was a great victory for our Warriors.

Upon our return I was given the shirt of a Lakota Warrior. To my surprise, on the front, my mother and sister had quilled the beautiful image of my best friend. In the years that followed, Storm and I shared many adventures—too many to tell. And so, with my Gift Horse, I rode from boyhood into manhood.

The one thing I will never forget from my early days, so long ago, is the horse with eagle feathers tied in her mane and the red handprint of a boy. I can still see the two of us riding across the endless prairies of our youth, like a hailstorm and a flying cloud.

Author's Note

My great-great grandfather's name was Flying Cloud, and he was a Lakota Warrior. I am a member of the Standing Rock Sioux Tribe in the Dakotas, descendants of the Lakota Indians about whom this story is told. Many times I have wondered what it was like for Flying Cloud, as a boy, growing up. That is how I came to write this tale. When I was a child, my mother, Christine-Elk Tooth Woman, often told me about the Old Ones who came before her, including Flying Cloud.

Lakota Indians are also known as the Sioux. This label, which means "snakes" in the most reviled sense of the word, was originally given to them by their Ojibwa [Chippewa] enemies. However, today, Sioux denotes the proud race of the Plains Indians still living in the Dakotas.

In the eighteenth and nineteenth centuries the Lakota lived on the vast grasslands of what is now the central part of the United States. Mounted on horses, they followed the great herds of buffalo that supplied them with most of their food and clothing, and even skins to cover their tipis. They lived as part of the natural world, integrating themselves into it. For guidance and understanding they called upon Wakan-Tanka, the Great Spirit, who is the life force that exists within all things. The Lakota lived in harmony with the changing seasons, with all of the other creatures, and with all of the different elements in their environment. Their manner of life reflected the lives around them; for instance, they hunted in bands much as wolves do. They revered all of Creation—Sun, Moon, Stars, Mother Earth—and called the four-legged beings and the winged creatures their brothers. To this

day, the Lakota believe that the green growing things are their relatives. A curious contradiction of humanity is that they did not always get along with their neighboring Indian tribes and were known as fierce warriors. In 1876 the Lakota and Cheyenne joined together to defeat General Custer at the Battle of Little Big Horn.

Horses were considered a sacred animal, and one of the finest gifts that a person could give to another. The Lakota painted their horses and decorated their own bodies as a symbolic connection to the natural world. Symbols could provide strength, protection, and supernatural powers. Thunderbolts signified "raw power," and the color red represented the rising Sun that is the Spirit of the East and wakens each day. Images of the dragonfly and lizard were used because those creatures were difficult to catch and kill. Both men and horses wore eagle feathers tied in their hair that gave them the "thunderbird" power of the winged ones. Similarly, wearing a headdress made with buffalo horns or a wolfskin would provide the Warrior with that animal's innate qualities.

A Lakota boy thirteen to sixteen years old underwent a rite of passage into manhood. This process was a means of preparing him to become a contributing member of the tribe. Many stages prepared a boy for this event.

The *sweat lodge* was used for spiritual purification. A sweat lodge was a low, domed structure made out of bent saplings, covered with buffalo hides or blankets. Inside, it was black as night and virtually airtight. When a participant entered the lodge, he was returning to the womb of Mother Earth. Participants sat in a circle. Sage, cedar, and sweet grass were burned as incense. Water poured over hot stones created steam. To participate in a sweat lodge was sacred—a time when prayers were said and answered. A *Vision Quest* was an individual's journey into the spirit world. Through fasting and meditation a person—isolated from the rest of the tribe—might receive insights. Some individuals received a vision for an entire lifetime.

To become a Warrior, a boy needed to be an accomplished hunter and possess at least one good horse, a bow and arrows, a shield, and a fine Warrior shirt. But most of all he needed courage. There was no greater demonstration of courage than *counting coup* against an enemy. This meant touching or striking an enemy with one's bow or even with one's bare hand. The intention was not to injure the enemy, but to make contact and escape unharmed. This was proof that one had achieved Warrior status. Flying Cloud counts coup when he knocks over the Crow guard and rides away unscathed.

The world has changed since this story of Flying Cloud. The Lakota and the Crow now consider each other friends. Today's Warriors are known by their words and deeds and gain honor by caring for their fellow human beings and the wild creatures. Today there is greater equity and shared responsibilities—both boys and girls compete in sporting events, create beadwork, and participate in sweat lodges as well as other rituals and traditions.

My illustrations are done with acrylic paint on wood panel. My style is directly influenced by the ledger book drawings (1865–1935) of Plains Indian artists. In my paintings I connect with Wakan-Tanka, the Great Spirit. I spread paint and color so that you might share in my vision. For I have an artist's vision of Father Sky and Mother Earth, of the winged ones, of our four-legged brothers, of the little crawling creatures, and the two-legged humans. I have a vision of the mountains and forests, all singing the song of life, all dancing in a circle, in a good way.

I would like to thank my wife, Karen, for choosing to dance in the circle with me. And I will be forever grateful to the keepers of the sweat lodge and to the Sun Dancers, Uncle Alan, Dicky, and Lindy for teaching me how to walk the Warrior's Path.

I wish to thank Rudy Rãmos for his early design consultation on the production of the artwork. Lastly, I would like to acknowledge my primary source of information, Colin F. Taylor, for his extensive research on Plains Indians.

Project Manager: Margaret L. Kaplan
Designer: Edward Miller

Library of Congress Cataloging-in-Publication Data
Nelson, S.D.
    Gift horse / S.D. Nelson
        p.   cm.
    Summary: Relates the story of a Lakota youth whose father gives him a horse in preparation for his making the transition from boyhood into manhood and becoming a Lakota Warrior.
    ISBN 0-8109-4127-9
    1. Dakota youth–Juvenile literature. 2. Horses–Great Plains–Juvenile literature.
    [1. Dakota Indians. 2. Indians of North America–Great Plains. 3. Horses.] I. Title
E99.D1N45   1999
978'.0049755'0092—dc21   98–51666

Published in 1999 by Harry N. Abrams, Incorporated, New York
All rights reserved. No part of the contents of this book may be reproduced without the written permission of the publisher.
Printed and bound in Hong Kong

ABRAMS   Harry N. Abrams, Inc.
100 Fifth Avenue
New York, N.Y. 10011
www.abramsbooks.com